ADAM SHARP
·Swimming with Sharks·

by George Edward Stanley
illustrated by Guy Francis

A STEPPING STONE BOOK™
Random House 🏠 New York

To JoAnn—the best sister
a brother could have
—G.E.S.

To Jake and Joey
—G.F.

Text copyright © 2003 by George Edward Stanley. Illustrations copyright © 2003 by Guy Francis. All rights reserved under International and Pan-American Copyright Conventions. Published in the United States by Random House Children's Books, a division of Random House, Inc., New York, and simultaneously in Canada by Random House of Canada Limited, Toronto.

www.randomhouse.com/kids

Library of Congress Cataloging-in-Publication Data
Stanley, George Edward.
Adam Sharp : swimming with sharks / by George Edward Stanley ; illustrated by Guy Francis. — 1st ed.
    p. cm. "A stepping stone book."
SUMMARY: When the world's ships start sinking, secret agent Adam Sharp investigates and discovers metal robot sharks are behind the attacks.
ISBN 0-307-26418-1 (pbk.) — ISBN 0-307-46418-0 (lib. bdg.)
[1. Spies—Fiction. 2. Ships—Fiction. 3. Robots—Fiction.] I. Francis, Guy, ill. II. Title.
PZ7.S78694 Ah 2003 [Fic]—dc21 2002151035

Printed in the United States of America   First Edition
10 9 8 7 6 5 4 3 2

Contents

1
Red Alert!

Adam Sharp dribbled the soccer ball down the field. He left the other players behind. Even in his tuxedo and patent leather shoes, Adam ran faster than anyone else.

Friendly Elementary School was playing its rival, Smugg Elementary School. The game was tied 1 to 1. There were only two minutes left.

Suddenly, Adam's watch beeped and a message appeared. He was needed at IM-8 Headquarters right away. That was because Adam wasn't just a student. He was also a secret agent.

Adam was still pretty far from the goal, but he had to score now.

He kicked the ball hard.

The crowd gasped.

The ball sailed over the head of the goalie and into the net.

Half of the crowd went wild.

Friendly Elementary School, 2! Smugg Elementary School, 1!

The referee blew his whistle. The game

was over. Adam's team started running toward him.

Adam ran the other way. He didn't have time to celebrate. "Sorry!" he shouted. "I have to see the Gifted and Talented Teacher now!"

There really wasn't a Gifted and Talented Program at his school. It was just a cover for IM-8.

Adam raced toward the school building. IM-8 Headquarters was in a secret room behind the janitor's closet.

T was waiting for him there. T was the head of IM-8.

Adam brushed the grass off his tuxedo

and straightened his bow tie. "What's the problem, sir?" he asked.

"The United Nations just called. There's a Red Alert," T said. "The secretary-general wants to see you right away, Sharp."

Adam shuddered. A Red Alert meant that the whole world was in trouble!

"I'm ready, sir!" Adam said. "I'm sure Mrs. Digby will let me make up my spelling test next week."

Adam followed T to the IM-8 helicopter parked on the roof of the school. They flew out of Friendly, Maryland, toward New York City.

The secretary-general met them when
they arrived. He took Adam to the General
Assembly Auditorium.

Adam sat next to the ambassador from
China. He waved to the queen of England.
The meeting began.

One by one, the world's leaders told

their stories. Something was sinking ships around the world. But no one knew what!

A Spanish ship had lost tons of olives. A Chinese ship had lost tons of chopsticks. An Australian ship had lost tons of boomerangs.

"Our ship lost tons of snowshoes," said the Russian ambassador. "Now the people

in Siberia can't leave their homes. They'll have to stay inside all winter and watch reruns of *I Love Lucy!*"

The world's leaders groaned.

Just then, someone handed Adam a message. "An American ship loaded with bubble gum is sinking off the U.S. coast," he read. "The president wants you to find out why."

It's happening again! Adam thought. He raced out of the auditorium and to the roof, where T was waiting.

"The world is counting on IM-8, T!" Adam cried. "We have to save the ships!"

2

Made in Bermuda

The IM-8 helicopter lifted off. It headed toward the Atlantic Ocean.

Adam put on flippers, a face mask, and an oxygen tank. He always kept them in the rear of the helicopter just in case.

Fifty miles off the U.S. coast, T spotted the sinking ship. Bubble gum was floating on top of the water.

"Where's the crew?" Adam asked.

"They've already been rescued," T said. "They're on their way back to port."

T lowered the helicopter until it was right above the water. Adam checked his gear again. He was ready.

"Now!" T shouted.

Adam plunged into the ocean. He started swimming underwater toward the ship. When he reached it, he saw why it was sinking. Three huge sharks were biting the bottom!

Adam knew danger lay ahead, but he swam closer anyway. "Fear" was a word IM-8 agents didn't know. In fact, Adam had even missed it on his last spelling test.

One of the sharks looked straight at Adam. It opened its big mouth. Adam had never seen such big teeth before.

The shark blew a big bubble and started swimming toward him. Adam pushed a black button on his watch.

It sent out a spray of shark repellent.

The shark kept coming.

I have to tell T we need a new shark repellent formula, thought Adam.

Adam aimed his watch at the shark and pushed a green button.

His watch sent out a message in shark language. It said, "Danger! Get out of here!"

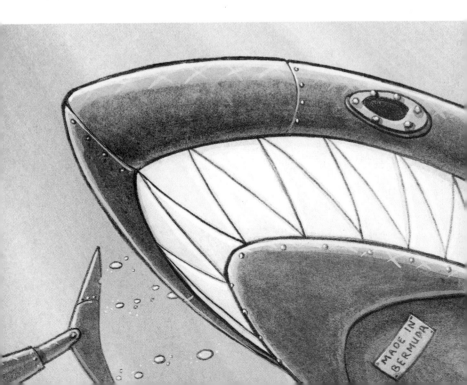

The shark came closer. It didn't seem to understand.

Then Adam noticed something. This shark didn't look . . . real. Adam could see where it was put together with rivets. These sharks were metal!

The shark did a somersault in the water. Adam gasped. There on its stomach were the words MADE IN BERMUDA.

3

Kay Largo

Quickly, Adam resurfaced. He saw the IM-8 helicopter hovering to his left. He pushed a red button on his watch. It sent a signal to T that he was ready to be picked up.

T guided the helicopter over Adam and dropped a cable. Adam hooked the cable to his suit, and T pulled him up.

Adam told T what he had seen. "We

need to go to Bermuda, sir," Adam added. "Who's our contact there?"

"Kay Largo, IM-8's top computer expert," T said. "She's also a champion surfer!"

Adam radioed Kay. He explained the mission to her. "I'll be there early tomorrow," he said.

"I'm stoked, dude!" Kay said.

Surfer talk, Adam thought. *I'd better look over the* IM-8 Surfer Dictionary *before we get there!*

The plane landed at sunrise. The airport was right on the beach.

"There's Kay now!" T said.

Adam looked. Kay was surfing in on a big wave. She wore a black wet suit and had a red flower behind her ear.

"Welcome to Bermuda, dude!" Kay called to Adam.

"Thanks," Adam said.

Kay propped up her surfboard and took off her wet suit. Underneath, she was wearing Bermuda shorts and a tank top. She put on a pair of flip-flops. "My disguise," she said.

Adam pulled a pair of sunglasses from the pocket of his tuxedo. "My disguise," he said.

"Let's go to IM-8 Headquarters, Bermuda. We need to make some plans!" Kay said. They were racing into town when Adam heard music.

"What's that?" he asked.

"It's a carnival," Kay replied.

A band came marching down the street. Hundreds of people in funny costumes followed it. They were laughing and singing and dancing.

Adam looked around. "Kay, there's no time to wait!" he shouted. "Is there any other way to cross the street?"

"No!" Kay shouted. "We have to cut through the parade!"

She pulled Adam into the line.

They started laughing and singing and dancing, too.

When the parade turned a corner, Kay dragged Adam into a narrow alley on the other side of the street.

"This way!" she said.

They ran down the alley, past a row of colorful houses, and into the town square. Lining the square were booths full of all sorts of stuff. One booth had olives. Another had chopsticks, and a third booth had boomerangs.

Hmm, Adam thought. "Let's check out this place, Kay," he said.

"Adam!" Kay said. "It's no time to be shopping at the flea market!"

"I'm only shopping for *clues,* Kay," Adam said. He went straight to a booth that had hundreds of snowshoes stacked in front of it.

"How many of these have you sold?" Adam asked the man in the booth.

"None," the man replied. "No one wears snowshoes in Bermuda. But I have to sell what *Finders Keepers* brings me."

"What is *Finders Keepers*?" Kay asked.

The man pointed to the harbor. "That boat," he said.

"Of course, Kay! A Russian ship carrying snowshoes sank. The people of Siberia have to stay inside all winter," Adam said. "We need to talk to the captain. I want to know where *Finders Keepers* got these snowshoes!"

But just as they reached the pier,

Finders Keepers tooted its horn and pulled away.

Adam and Kay ran back to the booth with the snowshoes. "Where is that boat going?" Adam asked.

"The flea market on the other side of the island. The captain's taking them a load of bubble gum," the man said. "Now, *that's* something I could sell!"

Adam looked at Kay. "We'll never get there in time."

"Dude!" Kay said. "Trust me!"

They ran down a narrow alley and through a gate. Adam saw a grass shack.

"Where are we?" he asked.

Kay gave Adam a funny look. "That shack is IM-8 Headquarters, Bermuda!" She propped her surfboard up against the shack.

Adam peeked inside. He saw lots of computers. "Cool," he said.

Two mopeds were leaning against the fence. Adam and Kay jumped on them and sped back down the alley.

"If we take the cliff road, we can totally keep an eye on *Finders Keepers*," Kay said.

Below them, *Finders Keepers* was staying near the shore as it sailed around the island.

Adam and Kay rode into a thick grove of trees. When they came out, they could no longer see the boat.

"No way!" Kay said. "*Finders Keepers* just disappeared!"

4

The Secret Cove

Adam looked around. "Is there someplace *Finders Keepers* could be hiding?" he asked.

Kay thought for a minute. "Dude! There's supposed to be a secret cove down there somewhere," she said. "But I've never been able to find it!"

"Come on, Kay! I'm good at finding

secret places!" Adam said. "I've found them all over the world!"

They parked their mopeds and started down the hill.

A few minutes later, Adam stopped. "Something feels wrong," he said.

"IM-8 Rule 1542," Kay said. "When something feels wrong, look for traps!"

"Of course!" Adam said. He grabbed a tree branch and pulled himself onto it. "Kay! This tree is plastic!" he said.

Kay checked out some of the other trees. "So are these!" she said. "Why would anybody put plastic trees on the side of a hill?"

Adam shrugged. He climbed to the top of the plastic tree and looked around. "No trap!" he reported.

They started down the hill again.

Just as they reached the beach, there was a loud rumble. Above them, the plastic trees had folded over.

"Check it out!" Kay said. "There's a crack in the side of the hill!"

Adam and Kay ran to the end of the beach to get a better look. All of a sudden, the hill began to open.

"The secret cove!" Kay said.

At that moment, a boat came sailing out. It was *Finders Keepers*!

So that's where it went, Adam thought.

When *Finders Keepers* was clear of the opening, the hill began to close.

"Quick, Kay!" Adam shouted. "We have to see what's inside!" He and Kay jumped in the water and swam toward the opening.

Kay was a really fast swimmer. Good thing Adam had practiced hard for his last IM-8 swimming test.

They swam inside just as the side of the hill closed. Adam looked around. They were in the middle of a lake inside a huge cavern.

On the far side of the cavern, there was a loading dock for boats.

Several men in strange uniforms were standing on the dock. They were putting big metal teeth into the mouth of a big metal shark!

5

Shark Factory

"Let's get closer," Adam whispered to Kay. They started swimming toward the dock.

Suddenly, alarms went off and bright lights came on overhead.

Adam and Kay stopped swimming and looked around. "What happened?" Kay whispered.

"We must have broken an underwater

electric beam and set off the alarms!"
Adam said.

"Well, well, well!" boomed a voice over
a loudspeaker. "Adam Sharp and Kay
Largo! Heh! Heh! Heh!"

"General Menace! My archenemy!"
Adam said. "I should have known he was
behind something this evil!"

A motorboat roared toward Adam and
Kay. Two men in strange uniforms pulled
them from the water and took them to
General Menace.

"So this is your evil headquarters!"
Adam said. "Why do you keep trying to
take over the world?"

"I want to make it a better place for evil!" General Menace said. "Heh! Heh! Heh!"

Adam looked around. "Is this where you make the sharks that have been biting the bottoms of ships?" he asked.

General Menace nodded proudly. "But that was just a trial run! In a few minutes, we'll send out a thousand sharks to finish the job!" he said. "Soon only *my* ships will sail the seas!"

"Dude! How do they know which ships to bite?" Kay asked. "Why don't they bite yours?"

"Computers, my dear! Computers!"

General Menace said. He pointed to a big gray computer. "We program the sharks so that they only bite other people's ships."

"No way!" Kay said. "That is so evil!"

"Heh! Heh! Heh!" said General Menace. "That's what I'm all about!"

Adam and Kay exchanged glances. In his head, Adam translated Kay's look. It said, "Keep General Menace busy!"

I can do that! Adam thought. *General Menace likes to brag!*

"Well, General Menace, you really outsmarted IM-8 this time!" Adam said in a loud voice. "Whose brilliant idea was this?"

General Menace puffed out his chest.

"Mine, of course! You see, one day when I was feeding my fish . . ."

While General Menace talked about how wonderful he was, Kay eased over to the big gray computer. Adam watched her out of the corner of his eye. Kay typed so fast that her hands were a blur.

I hope she's as good as T said, Adam thought grimly.

When Kay finished, she eased back over to where General Menace and Adam were standing.

Just then, a soldier in a strange uniform came over and whispered into General Menace's ear.

"Heh! Heh! Heh! It's time to release the sharks!" General Menace said.

The soldier typed a command on the big gray computer. A large gate on one side of the cavern opened. A thousand sharks swam out.

"Bon voyage!" General Menace called.

He looked at Adam. "That's French for 'Have a good trip!'"

"I know," Adam said. "I speak several languages."

The hill split open, and the sharks swam into the ocean.

"Now we're going to watch television," General Menace said. He led Adam and Kay to a large television set. A map of the world filled the screen. There were flashing red and green lights in all the oceans.

"What are those lights for?" Adam asked.

"The green lights are my ships. The red lights are everybody else's ships," General Menace said. "We're going to watch the red lights go out one by one."

"This is so boring," Kay said. "Let's watch the Surfing Channel instead."

Suddenly, a green light went out.

General Menace gasped.

Three more green lights went out.

"What's happening?" screamed General Menace.

"Look!" Adam shouted. "*All* the green lights are going out!"

"It worked!" Kay cheered.

General Menace scowled at her. "What did you do?" he demanded.

"I reprogrammed your computer, General Menace. The sharks are biting the bottoms of *your* ships!" Kay said. "Your evil work here is finished!"

"Never!" screamed General Menace. He and his soldiers ran toward the big gray computer.

"Kay!" Adam whispered. "He's going to reprogram it."

Kay grinned. "It's too late," she said. "But let's get out of here before he figures that out!"

Adam and Kay jumped into the water and started swimming. They were halfway to the opening when General Menace shouted, "STOP THEM!"

That made Adam and Kay swim even faster.

General Menace's soldiers roared after them in two motorboats.

Adam looked over his shoulder. The motorboats were gaining on them.

Just then, a really big shark surfaced between the two boats. It headed right toward them!

"Swim, Kay, swim!" Adam shouted.

But the shark was too fast. It opened its huge jaws and swallowed up Adam and Kay!

Inside the shark's mouth, it was darker than dark. Adam quickly pushed a yellow button on his watch. The watch gave off a glow.

"There's no escape, Kay!" Adam said. "We're doomed!"

Kay leaned back. "Chill out, Adam!" she said. "When I was messing with

General Menace's computer, I programmed
one of the sharks to pick us up. It's going
to spit us out on the beach!"

Suddenly, the shark hiccuped.

"Hold on!" Kay shouted.

Adam and Kay went flying through the air. They landed in a soft pile of sand.

"Wow!" Adam said. "That was amazing!"

"I know," said Kay. "But I'm sure General Menace will turn up again."

Adam pushed a button on his watch. He filled T in on what had happened.

"Great job, Sharp! Great job, Largo!" T's voice said. "Take the rest of the day off. I'll pick you up at sunset."

Adam turned to tell Kay the good news. But Kay was digging in the sand with a big shell.

"What are you doing?" Adam asked.

"Building a sand castle," Kay said. She grinned at him. "I'm also IM-8's champion sand castle builder."

Adam hadn't even known IM-8 had a sand castle test. He was sure he could build a great sand castle, too. He grabbed a shell and started digging.

When T arrived at sunset, he could judge which sand castle was better!